SLAM CITY

PAPERCUTZ

OTHER GREAT GRAPHIC NOVELS AVAILABLE FROM PAPERCUTZ

#1 "FINISHED!"

Mathias Triton – Writer
Alitha E. Martinez – Artist
JayJay Jackson – Colorist

New York

WWE SLAM CITY
#1 "Finished!"

Mathias Triton – Writer
Alitha E. Martinez – Artist
Jolyon Yates – Cover Artist
JayJay Jackson – Colorist
Tom Orzechowski – Letterer
Dawn K. Guzzo – Production
Beth Scorzato – Production Coordinator
Michael Petranek – Associate Editor
Eric Lyga, Steven Pantaleo – Special Thanks

Jim Salicrup
Editor-in-Chief

ISBN: 978-1-59707-721-7 paperback edition
ISBN: 978-1-59707-722-4 hardcover edition

Papercutz books may be purchased for business or promotional use. For information on bulk purchases
please contact Macmillan Corporate and Premium Sales Department at (800) 221-7945 x5442.

Printed in the USA
August 2014 by Lifetouch Printing
5126 Forest Hills Ct.
Loves Park, IL 61111

Distributed by Macmillan
First Printing

*ASAP = AS SOON AS POSSIBLE.

THE NEXT DAY, AT THE *GREASY LUBE* ACROSS TOWN...

THANK YOU FOR THE OPPORTUNITY, SIR. I WON'T LET YOU DOWN.

GREASY LUBE

GREASY LUBE

HELP WANTED

YEAH, YEAH, YEAH, JOHN. JUST REMEMBER TWO THINGS I EXPECT FROM MY EMPLOYEES: FIX THE CARS, AND DON'T MAKE A MESS.

UNDER-STOOD, SIR.

AND DON'T CALL ME "SIR." IT'S MR. GREASY, LIKE ON THE SIGN OUTSIDE.

YES, SI-- ER, MR. GREASY? REALLY?

OF COURSE! WHERE DO YOU THINK I GOT THE NAME FOR THE PLACE?

NOW I'VE GOT A HOT DATE TONIGHT, SO YOU'RE CLOSING UP. TRY NOT TO DESTROY THE PLACE.

YES, MR. GREASY.

LOOK MR. MYSTERIO, MR. KANE, I'LL BE HONEST. I DON'T HAVE A LOT OF EXPERIENCE PLACING EX-SUPERSTARS IN JOBS. WHAT DO YOU LIKE TO DO?

JUMPING AROUND AND KICKING GUYS IN THE CHEST!

SMASHING FACES IN?

≶SIGH.≶ I MEANT *OUTSIDE* THE RING.

SO DID WE.

YEAH.

OKAY, I JUST GOT THESE POSTINGS IN FROM THE ELEMENTARY SCHOOL. THEY'RE DESPERATE-- THEY NEED PEOPLE RIGHT AWAY. YOU INTERESTED?

WORKING WITH KIDS? SURE!

≶GRRR.≶ ISN'T THERE ANYTHING ELSE?

COME ON-- HOW BAD COULD IT BE?

MEANWHILE, BACK AT *WWE* HEADQUARTERS...

MWAH-HA-HA! NOW THAT THESE CHUMPS ARE ALL GONE, I CAN TAKE MY RIGHTFUL PLACE AS THE UNDISPUTED CHAMPION OF THE *WWE!*

YES, SIR!

ABSOLUTELY, SIR!

HE CAN DO THAT? JUST ANOINT HIMSELF CHAMPION?

WAIT. SOMETHING'S WRONG. SOMETHING'S MISSING. THERE'S SOMETHING THEY ALL HAVE THAT I DON'T.

POOR HYGIENE?

BAD TASTE IN CLOTHING?

SELF-RESPECT?

THE CHAMPIONSHIP!

TO BE A TRUE CHAMPION, I MUST HAVE IT! WE MUST FIND IT! I WILL LOOK HERE-- YOU THREE, COMB THE CITY FOR IT. LITERALLY, *COMB THE CITY!*

OH-A, POOR SANTINO. WHAT WILL YOU DO? EATING IS NO JOB AND THE COBRA KNOWS-A NOTHING ELSE BUT BEING THE COBRA!

GREASY LUBE

I WONDER IF-A JOHN COULD-A USE-A SOME HELP.

WHAPP

YOU THINK YOU'RE SO TOUGH, MR. BIG SHOT CENA. LET'S SEE HOW YOU HANDLE...

THIS!

THWAKK

OHO, SHIFTY AREN'T YOU? WELL, YOU KNOW WHAT THEY SAY?

THIRD TIME'S THE CH--

SIR!

JUST AT THAT MOMENT...

SILLY SANTINO. GET ALL-A THE WAY TO THE ZOO AND FORGET THE GIANT-SIZED COMB. HOW AM I SUPPOSED TO COMB-A THE GIRAFFE?

OH, HERE IT-- MAMA MIA! WHAT IS THIS? THAT'S-A MY FRIEND JOHN CENA'S ARM PROTRUDING FROM THAT-A MASS OF HUMANITY!

I WILL-A SAVE YOU!

CRONCH

OWW!

WATCH OUT FOR PAPERCUTZ™

Welcome to power-packed, premiere WWE SLAM CITY graphic novel from Papercutz, those pencil-neck geeks who are dedicated to publishing great graphic novels for all ages! I'm Jim Salicrup, the Editor-in-Chief and retired SLAM CITY referee.

It's been a real thrill putting this all-new graphic novel together, based on the WWE SLAM CITY animated short films that have been playing all over the world-wide web! The WWE SLAM CITY creative crew has been a real pleasure to work with, but there was one odd aspect to that I'd like to share with you. You see, our writer is something of an enigma. In fact, I haven't actually met him in-person, and he tends to be rather secretive. Anxious to learn more about him, we asked him to send us a short bio that we could post here to share with the WWE Universe. Here it is…

"Who is Mathias Triton? Hero or villain? Champ or chump? No one knows for sure. This man of mystery claims to be a New York Times best-selling author, an accomplished graphic novel writer, and the only man ever to beat Andre the Giant in a fair fight. But which of these facts are true? Perhaps all. Perhaps none. The only thing we know for sure is that he has his checks sent directly to a one-man bank in Gammesfeld, Germany."

That bio actually raises more questions than it answers. I mean, I have enough problems trying to figure out who the Instigator is. Fortunately, I do know who Alitha E. Martinez is! She's the artist who did such an awesome job illustrating the first four issues of the WWE SUPERSTARS comicbook from Super Genius, a Papercutz imprint. All four issues have been collected into a trade paperback called WWE SUPERSTARS #1 "Money in the Bank!" and is available now at booksellers everywhere for just $9.99! It features all your favorite WWE Superstars in a story that shows them in a way you've never seen them

before—as characters in a noir thriller. Alitha did such an amazing job drawing so many WWE superstars, and their signature moves, that we couldn't think of anyone better qualified to draw WWE SLAM CITY! (Somehow, Alitha managed to find enough time in her busy schedule to do a very special sequence, as well as the cover to issue #7 of WWE SUPERSTARS. It's in yet another style than we've already seen from this talented artist!)

We're also lucky to know who JayJay Jackson and Tom Orzechowski are—they also worked away on WWE SUPERSTARS, handling the coloring and lettering respectively. When you have such top talents available, why look for anyone else? So, we're thrilled to have them work on WWE SLAM CITY as well!

We're all having such fun on this graphic novel, we're going to do it all over again! That's right, this is not just a one-shot, but an on-going series of WWE SLAM CITY graphic novels! Up next is "WWE SLAM CITY #2 "Rise of El Diablo"! Just to whet your appetite, we're featuring a special preview on the following pages—so check it out! In the meantime, let us know what you thought WWE SLAM CITY #1! You can reach us via the contacts listed in the box below!

So until we meet again, as one of my favorite sports entertainers often says…

Have a nice day!

STAY IN TOUCH!

EMAIL: salicrup@papercutz.com
WEB: papercutz.com
TWITTER: @papercutzgn
FACEBOOK: PAPERCUTZGRAPHICNOVELS
FAN MAIL: Papercutz, 160 Broadway, Suite 700,
            East Wing, New York, NY 10038

Papercutz Editor-in-Chief Jim Salicrup meets WWE Legend (and erstwhile GI Joe) Sgt. Slaughter!

HAHAHAHA

DON'T FORGET THE KETCHUP!

JUUUUST RIGHT.

WAS IT SOMETHING I SAAAAAAIIIIIIID?

PRETZELS

MOMMY, MOMMY! REY MYSTERIO!

OKAY, HOW MUCH FOR THE LUCHADOR-SHAPED PRETZEL?

THAT'S AN EXTRA FIFTY CENTS.

STICKS

WHOA, FELLAS! I JUST CAME HERE TO HAVE SOME LUNCH TODAY. I'M NOT LOOKING FOR ANY TROUBLE.

YOU SHOULD HAVE THOUGHT OF THAT BEFORE YOU GOT ALL CRAZY WITH THE CONDIMENTS.

NICE ALLITERATION, BROCK.

NICE WHAT?

ALLITERATION. YOU KNOW, TWO WORDS THAT START WITH THE SAME LETTER?

OH, YOU MEAN LIKE COOKIES AND CAKE?

SURE. I GUESS.

AND CUP-CAKES?

ARE YOU TWO GOING TO STAND THERE LIKE MARAUDING MONKEYS OR ARE YOU GOING TO ATTACK ME?

SEE, MARAUDING MONKEYS, THAT WAS PRETTY GOOD TOO.

I GET IT NOW.

TWO BRUTES ATTACKING A HELPLESS VICTIM? NOT ON MY WATCH. NOT ON THE WATCH OF...